BOARDING-SCHOOL
BLUES

adapted by Kim Ostrow
illustrated by Robert Roper

POCKET
BOOKS

Pocket Books/Nickelodeon

New York   London   Toronto   Sydney   Singapore

POCKET
BOOKS

First published in Great Britain in 2003 by Pocket Books.
An imprint of Simon & Schuster UK Ltd
Africa House, 64-78 Kingsway, London WC2B 6AH

Originally published in 2002 by Simon Spotlight, an imprint of Simon & Schuster
Children's Publishing Division, New York.

A CIP catalogue record for this book is available from the British Library

ISBN 07434 61487

Printed and bound by Scotprint, Haddington

1 3 5 7 9 10 8 6 4 2

The Thornberrys sat around the Commvee like they did most nights – but this night was far from ordinary. Eliza had just risked her life racing through the plains of Africa to save a cheetah cub named Tally from poachers. Her parents made her promise she would leave saving animals to the park rangers.

"I promise," Eliza said sadly. But the poachers still had Tally.

"Yeah, right," said Debbie. "She's always sneaking off. . . ."
Eliza glared at Debbie.

"Hey, I've covered long enough!" Debbie said. "Do you know she once fed protein bars to a Komodo dragon and rode a Siberian tiger?"

"Eliza! Is this true?" Marianne asked. Eliza looked down at her feet.

"Nigel, Marianne," Eliza's grandmother Cordelia announced, "Eliza needs to be in a structured environment – such as Lady Beatrice's Boarding School in London."

"What about me?" Debbie shrieked. "I want to go too!"

Later that night Marianne looked at a picture of Eliza. "Are we doing the right thing?" she asked Nigel. "It's our only choice," he responded. "Eliza is not going to listen to reason when it comes to traipsing off into the wild. She's quite fearless, you know." "She takes after her father." Marianne sighed.

The moment Eliza arrived at Lady Beatrice's, she missed her family, the wild, and talking to animals – especially talking to Darwin.

"Remember, dear, I'm on the board of directors. Do me proud," said Cordelia, waving good-bye.

The schoolgirls stared as Eliza dragged along her heavy bag.

Eliza threw her bag onto her bed. Suddenly a voice from inside the bag yelled, "That's it! One more bump and you'll have a scrambled chimp!" Eliza ripped open her bag and out popped Darwin! Eliza gasped, and they hugged.

"You can't be here," Eliza said. The doorknob jiggled. "Oh, no! Someone's coming!" she whispered, and pushed him into the wardrobe.

Eliza rushed to the door and opened it. "Hi, I'm Eliza Thornberry," she said, out of breath. "Guess we're roommates."

"So it appears. I'm Sarah Wellington," the girl said snootily.

Sarah looked across the room. "I see you've already been in my wardrobe!" Then she went to examine the partly opened wardrobe door.

"Wait!" Eliza quickly shouted. "Want one of my mum's homemade peanut-butter cookies?"

Sarah stopped in her tracks. "I might have use for you yet," she said.

A week later, Eliza found some squirrels to talk to.

"It's great to talk to you guys. It's been awful." Eliza sighed.

"Go on, Eliza, tell Reggie your troubles," said the largest squirrel.

"I just miss my family and friends in Africa. I don't even know if they found the poachers who took my friend Tally!"

Just then Sarah and her friends walked by with their noses in the air.

"I heard she lived in the jungle and bathed where animals drank," said Sarah. "Next she'll bring animals into our room," she added.

Eliza did her best to ignore them.

The dinner bell rang and Eliza headed towards the cafeteria.

"We are a little curious," said Victoria, one of the girls who sat near Eliza. "Have you ever seen a tiger?"

"Actually, I've seen lots of tigers," said Eliza proudly.

"Tell us more, Eliza!" said Victoria.

Just then a strange-looking girl sat down. It was Darwin dressed in Sarah's clothes!

"Don't I look fetching?" he whispered to Eliza.

"Who's that girl? I've never seen her before," said Jane.

Then Sarah noticed something very familiar about Darwin's uniform. "That's my blazer!"

Sarah began to tug on the sleeves of Darwin's jacket and noticed how hairy his arm was! Darwin tugged back and his hat fell off. Sarah shrieked.

"It's a chimpanzee!" someone shouted. The cafeteria erupted with squeals and cheers. Milk and mashed potatoes flew through the air. "This is the best dinner we've ever had!" said Victoria.

Darwin was put in a horse stall with a nice horse named Thunder.
Back in her room Eliza told her new friends all about poor Tally.

Victoria wanted to write letters to help save Tally. Jane suggested a
bake sale. Eliza just wanted to get Darwin and go home.

Then Sarah came back from brushing her teeth. "You'll all have to
go," she snapped. "I've been at Mrs Fairgood's all evening filling out a
report and I'm quite tired."

Disappointed, the girls filed out of the room and off to bed.

That night, Eliza had a dream. She was walking around the school. Suddenly an elephant ran by her. She was back in Africa! Then Eliza saw another animal out of the corner of her eye – it was Tally!

"Eliza! Help!" he shouted.

Next a shadow appeared.

It was Shaman Mnyambo – the man who had given Eliza the gift of speaking to animals.

"You have a greater destiny, Eliza," he whispered. "You must go to it."

"What do you mean?" asked Eliza.

"Go, Eliza," he said. "Go! GO!"

Then a dark hole appeared in the ground. Eliza began to fall. . . .

"Tally's alive!" Eliza shouted as she ran to the wardrobe to get her bag.

"What are you doing?" Sarah yawned. She rubbed her eyes.

"I have to leave," said Eliza. Tally needed her help!

"I'm telling Mrs Fairgood," Sarah said, heading for the door.

"No, please," begged Eliza.

"You have to keep this a secret. Do you have a credit card? I need two tickets to Africa."

"Africa? I am not taking part in this," Sarah said.

"Please. It's a matter of life and death. And you'll get your room back."

Sarah smiled. She headed straight for the phone and dialled. "Would you prefer a window or aisle seat?" she asked.

"Let's go," whispered Eliza, yanking Darwin out of the horse stall. They travelled quickly through the night.

Once they safely boarded the aeroplane, Darwin was happy to relax – and eat snacks.

   "We're going to save Tally, I just know it!" Eliza exclaimed.

   "Haven't we been through this already?" Darwin rolled his eyes.

   "Yeah," said Eliza, "but that was before I learnt about my destiny."

   "Here we go again," Darwin said and popped a peanut in his mouth.